The Big Toe
Robbery

The Big Toe Robbery

Story by Trevor Todd

Illustrations by Craig Smith

PM Chapter Books
part of the Rigby PM Collection

U.S. edition © 2001 Rigby
a division of Reed Elsevier Inc.
500 Coventry Lane
Crystal Lake, IL 60014
www.rigby.com

Text © 2001 Nelson Thomson Learning
Illustrations © 2001 Nelson Thomson Learning
Originally published in Australia by Nelson Thomson Learning

06 05 04 03 02 01
10 9 8 7 6 5 4 3 2 1

The Big Toe Robbery
ISBN 0 7635 7795 2

Printed in China by Midas Printing (Asia) Ltd

Contents

Chapter 1

A Wonderful Idea

Justin's favorite class was art. His teacher, Ms. Winter, said he had talent. But today it was too hot to draw and the afternoon seemed to drag on forever. Ms. Winter was upset. All the other students had their heads down and were busy drawing, but Justin just sat at his desk. He didn't like this extreme heat. It sapped his energy.

"Justin," implored Ms. Winter. "This is not like you! You're usually the first to finish—and you haven't even started!"

"Sorry, Ms. Winter," sighed Justin. "It's the heat. I can't think of anything to draw."

"Well, just draw the first thing that comes into your head," snapped Ms. Winter. Obviously, the heat was getting to her, too. Usually, she was the most pleasant teacher in the whole school.

Justin wriggled his toes. His big toe was sticking out of his right sock and sneaker. His mother had pleaded with him to let her buy him some new sneakers. But Justin liked these old ones, even though they were well past their "use-by" date.

The big toe on Justin's right foot was different. It was longer than usual for a big toe, but in the middle, it suddenly bent out to the left. Justin hadn't damaged his toe playing sports and the big toe on his left foot was like other people's big toes. He had just been born with a toe like that.

Suddenly Justin smiled to himself. Well, Ms. Winter did say to draw anything.

Ms. Winter glanced over at Justin and immediately felt relieved. At last, the boy was working away furiously. But later, when she wandered up to the back of the classroom and looked over Justin's shoulder, she was taken by surprise. There it was in all its glory: Justin's big toe. Ms. Winter wanted to laugh but stopped herself. There was something about the big toe that was— wonderful!

It had a bold outline, and just like Justin's big toe, it was long and curved to the left in the middle. But it was more than just a good likeness. It had a certain something. The big toe drawing seemed to say proudly, "Here I am! This is me! Like me or hate me, I don't care!" But a big toe drawing couldn't say all that! Could it?

"Justin…" The other kids in the class stopped working and looked up. "That's… good. No, it's better than good…it's amazing!" Ms. Winter turned to the rest of the class. "Look, everyone. Justin's done it again!"

The rest of the class left their seats and gathered around Justin's desk. There it was—his big toe. But there was something about it. Something that made people smile, that made people feel good.

The class murmured a mixture of disbelief and congratulations. How did he do it? Becky Squires looked at the big toe drawing. It seemed to dazzle her. She was doing some hard thinking.

"Justin, can I take your drawing home for the weekend?" she asked.

"Sure," answered Justin, handing her the sheet of paper.

Becky clutched the picture to her chest. She had an idea. It was too crazy to tell anyone, but it might help her save some more money for summer camp.

Chapter 2
Becky's Plan

As Becky made her way into Thornhill's Prints and Posters store that afternoon, she had a gleam in her eye. She had to wait because Mr. Thornhill was busy trying to please an angry customer. The laminated plastic on a family photograph was peeling off and the customer was furious.

"I'll have it fixed in a jiffy. Come back this time tomorrow," smiled Mr. Thornhill, showing his crooked teeth. His large stomach bulged over his belt. He gave an exaggerated friendly wave as the unhappy customer stormed out of the store. "You have a good day, now!"

He turned his attention to Becky and the smile died quickly. Becky took out Justin's drawing and slipped it across the counter toward Mr. Thornhill.

"I'd like some photocopies of this, please."

Mr. Thornhill glanced down at the big toe. He scowled. "Whatever for?"

"I ... kind of like it," answered Becky, her feelings of dislike for the man growing every second.

"Hmm," sniffed Mr. Thornhill. "Waste of paper. But you're paying. How many?"

Becky jutted out her chin. "A hundred reduced copies and a hundred at the same size."

Mr. Thornhill looked surprised.

"Some people have got more money than sense. Still, I'll do them now. While you're waiting have a look at my new collection of cards. Over there."

Becky glanced across at the display in the corner of the store.

"'Flowers of Spring'. Designed them myself. Birthday cards and invitations."

Mr. Thornhill busied himself at the photocopy machine. He messed up the first photocopy and put it to one side.

Becky wandered over to the display. The Flowers of Spring designs were truly terrible. The drawings of the flowers were so boring! There was nothing new or exciting about them at all. They didn't make you feel good—they just made you want to go to sleep.

"Great, aren't they?" called Mr. Thornhill from the photocopy machine.

Becky swallowed. What could she say? "Aaah … interesting … " she lied.

Mr. Thornhill came back to the counter with the photocopies in his hand.

"Tell all your friends at school."

"Hmm," she said, paid him the money, then fled from the store.

As Becky walked though the shopping mall with Justin's big toe pictures clutched tightly to her chest, she felt sure she was going to be able to save up enough money for that summer camp.

Chapter 3

Business Success

"Unreal!" said Justin enthusiastically.

Becky beamed. She had worked hard all weekend. The other kids wandered up, took one look at what Becky was holding, and were just as excited. There they were— the Big Toe cards and invitations, with Justin's big toe on the front. Surely, no one else had ever produced stationery before with such an unusual picture on the front!

"I'll take two. How much are they?" asked Robbie.

"I'll take ten," said Peter Salter. "My birthday's in two weeks and I'll use these as invitations. They're great!"

In no time, Becky had sold about half the cards. And that was without even trying! She took Justin to one side and whispered in his ear, "Fifty-fifty. What do you say?"

"What do you mean?" asked Justin.

"I'll make the cards and the invitations, and we'll split the profits equally. It's only fair as your big toe picture is the reason they're selling."

"I don't have to do anything else?" smiled Justin. Becky shook her head.

"Deal!" laughed Justin. They shook hands.

Becky and Justin were so excited by the success of the cards they could hardly believe it was happening. They made arrangements to set up a small folding table in the shopping mall to sell their collection of Big Toe cards and invitations. In just two hours they had almost sold out.

Justin's big toe picture had a magical effect on people. It made people feel good. It made them happy. It was so outrageously silly that people couldn't stop themselves from smiling.

But there was one person who was less than happy with the Big Toe success—Mr. Thornhill. His Flowers of Spring cards sat untouched on the shelves. No one was interested in them. He'd spent quite a lot of money creating his new cards, and those stupid toe cards were selling as fast as people could carry them away. He'd have to do something, or he'd be left with Flowers of Spring right through the summer, autumn, and winter, too.

Chapter 4

Mr. Thornhill Steals a Toe

Becky was tired. She'd been up half the night making more cards and invitations. She couldn't explain the success of Justin's drawing. People just loved it, and that was all that mattered. She walked into the mall and her eyes widened in surprise. She nearly dropped what she was carrying.

As if in a trance, Becky wandered over to Thornhill's Prints and Posters store. There was Justin's big toe picture on cards, but displayed in Mr. Thornhill's store window.

When Mr. Thornhill saw her coming, he looked embarrassed, but then stuck his jaw out and folded his arms. He looked at the dazed girl from behind his counter.

"How could you … ?" sputtered Becky.

"Listen, kid, a toe's a toe, a knee's a knee, and an elbow's an elbow. You can't copyright nature!"

"But it's Justin's design—and his toe!"

"Well, you've learned a lesson, kid. Life isn't fair. Now beat it. I've got work to do!"

"Yes!" spat Becky. "Dirty work!"

Mr. Thornhill looked at the ceiling. He was guilty of stealing Justin's design, and he knew it. But there was no way Becky was going to get him to admit it.

"Cheat!" she shouted, and her voice echoed across the shopping mall.

Chapter 5

The Protest

Mr. Thornhill looked up from counting the money in his cash register. There was a disturbance coming from the far corner of the shopping mall. Then the noise grew louder. It was coming his way. He gulped.

Becky Squires and Peter Salter were leading a pack of protesting classmates. They had banners. They were shouting. They were chanting. And, propped up on their shoulders, was Justin. His feet were bare. Every now and again the protesters would hold up Justin's right foot and chant:

"Oh, no! Oh, no! Mr. Thornhill stole Justin's toe!"

Mr. Thornhill rushed to the front of his store and tried to close the door. But he was too late. The kids filled the store. Other shoppers had gathered around, wondering what the noise was about.

Becky raised her arms and the protesters quieted. She turned to Mr. Thornhill. The sweat patches under his arms were twice the size they normally were, and his mouth was twitching. He looked very worried. More people had gathered. This was bad for business.

"Mr. Thornhill, we charge you with stealing Justin's big toe!"

All the kids shouted out "Yeah" in unison. Everyone looked at Mr. Thornhill. He looked at the adults staring at him through the store window.

"Look, a toe's a toe, an elbow's an elbow. How do you know it's this kid's toe?"

Becky smiled in triumph.

"Because..." She grabbed Justin's right foot and held it up for all the world to see. "There's only one toe like this—and it's Justin's!"

Everyone craned forward to see Justin's toe. And they saw that it was true. Justin's big toe was extraordinarily long, but more than that, it bent to the left. Surely, no one else had a toe just like that!

"I reckon the kid's right!" said a man in a red sweater. Others agreed. "Yeah!"

The kids started chanting again.

Mr. Thornhill could see that he was beaten.

"All right! All right!" he said, holding up his hands. "So, I might have accidentally copied the kid's drawing."

The kids booed. The adults joined in.

"Tell you what. You can have fifty percent of every toe design I sell. Okay?"

Becky smiled in triumph. "Sixty!"

Mr. Thornhill went white and muttered, "Deal."

Becky turned to the group of kids.

"Okay, everyone! It's ice-cream cones all around—and Mr. Thornhill's paying!"

She turned to Mr. Thornhill, who was now a quivering mess of a man. "Right?"

Mr. Thornhill nodded. The crowd of excited kids cheered. They streamed out of Thornhill's Prints and Posters store and descended on the ice cream parlor.

Mr. Thornhill shook his head and picked up one of the Big Toe cards. He'd never understand it. How could people prefer Justin's big toe picture to his Flowers of Spring designs? Life just wasn't fair!